You Be You

by Linda Kranz

TAYLOR TRADE PUBLISHING
Lanham • New York • Boulder • Toronto • Plymouth, UK

Published by TAYLOR TRADE PUBLISHING

An imprint of The Rowman & Littlefield Publishing Group, Inc.
4501 Forbes Boulevard, Suite 200, Lanham, Maryland 20706
http://www.rlpgtrade.com

Estover Road, Plymouth PL6 7PY, United Kingdom

Distributed by National Book Network

Text and illustrations copyright © 2011 by Linda Kranz
Designed by Maria Kauffman
Photography by Klaus Kranz

British Library Cataloguing in Publication Information Available

Library of Congress Cataloging-in-Publication Data
Kranz, Linda.
You be you / by Linda Kranz.
p. cm.
ISBN 978-1-58979-666-9 (cloth) — ISBN 978-1-58979-667-6 (electronic)
[1. Individuality—Fiction. 2. Self-acceptance—Fiction. 3. Fishes—Fiction.] I. Title.
PZ7.K8597Yo 2011
[E]—dc23
2011013350

Printed in Huizhou, Guangdong, PRC, China December 2014

For Sue L.

Thank you for your enthusiasm and friendship.

—L.K.

Adri bounced. He glided.
The expression on his face was pure joy.
He had been out all day exploring,
and now he was swimming home.

As he made his way through the ocean waves,
he couldn't help but notice that . . .

Some fish swim left.

Some fish swim right.

some fish

swim in a circle.

Some fish swim in a line.

Some fish swim up.
Some fish swim down.

some fish swim quiet.

SOME FISH SWIM LOUD.

Some fish are colorful.

some fish are plain.

Some fish look different.

Some fish look the same.

some fish are **BIG**.

some fish are tiny.

Some fish are smooth.

Some fish are spiny.

Some fish swim high.

Some fish swim low.

Some fish
swim together.

some fish swim

alone.

Some fish are RED.

Some fish are BLUE.

some fish swim
in the sunshine.

some fish swim
by the moon.

Mama and Papa beamed when Adri arrived.

He was excited to tell them what he had discovered in his travels.
Mama and Papa listened eagerly as he told them about all of the fish that he saw.

"There are so many of us!" Adri said.
"We all have something special that only we can share."

Papa agreed. "We can learn so much from each other."
He smiled. "There are millions of fish in the deep blue sea.
That's what makes the world so colorful and beautiful!"

"Life is a grand journey, Adri," Mama said.

"You be you."

SWIM!

Share

you are an original

CHOOSE HAPPINESS

Be inspired

If the waters turn choppy ~ float

make a difference

Be excited

Focus on those things that make you come alive

Always be the best you can be

savor moments of joy

Notice kindness

Simply live your best life every day

Surround yourself with amazing uplifting friends

Constantly think of new ways to reinvent yourself

FIND YOUR BLISS

Notice the colors in the sky at sunset

Have fun

Take care of your heart

RECEIVED FEB - - 2016

Laugh more, worry less